RIVER

RIVER AND BRIDGE

poems by

MEENA ALEXANDER

TSAR
Toronto
Oxford
1996

The publishers acknowledge generous assistance
from the Ontario Arts Council and the Canada Council.

© 1996 Meena Alexander

Except for purposes of review, no part of this book may be reproduced
in any form without prior permission of the publisher.

First published in 1995 by Rupa (New Delhi, India). A few poems have
been slightly revised for this edition.
FIRST NORTH AMERICAN EDITION

Author photo by Colleen McKay
Cover art: woodcut "River and Bridge" by Zarina

Canadian Cataloguing in Publication Data

Alexander, Meena, 1951-
    River and bridge

Poems.
ISBN 0-920661-56-4

I. Title.

PR9499.3.A46R58 1996   811'.54   C96-931793-X

Printed in Canada

TSAR Publications
P.O. Box 6996, Station A
Toronto, M5W 1X7 Canada

Look I have burnt my house
I shall burn the house of anyone who follows!
                                    KABIR

Acknowledgement

Acknowledgement is gratefully made to the journals and anthologies in which these poems appeared.

Amerasia Journal: "San Andreas Fault"; "Moving World"
Ariel: "Elephants in Heat"
Arc: "Room without Walls"
Bombay Literature Review: "Ashtamudi Lake"
Chicago Review: "Estrangement Becomes the Mark of the Eagle"; "Desert Rose"
Conditions: "Blood Line"; "Toxic Petals"
Contemporary Indian Poetry: An Anthology, Ohio University Press: "Everything Strikes Loose"; "South of the Nilgiris"
Denver Quarterly: "Revelation"
Grand Street: "Paper Filled with Light"
Kavya Bharati (India): "Prison Cell"; "Mandala"; "Muse"
The Literary Review: "Deer Park at Sarnath"; "Landscape with Door"
Massachusetts Review: "Passion"; "Under the Incense Tree"; "Softly my Soul"
Michigan Quarterly Review: "Asylum"
New Letters: "No Man's Land"
Nimrod: "Lost Language"; "Indian Sandstone"
The Poetry Review (London): "River and Bridge"; "Art of Pariahs"
The Portable Lower East Side: "News of the World"; "Against Elegy"; "Brown Skin, What Mask?"
Quarry West: "Sweet Water"
River Styx: "Skin Song"
The Toronto South Asian Review: "City Street"; "For Safdar Hashmi"; "Moloyashree"
World Literature Today: "Sweet Alyssum"
Yatra (India): "No Witnesses"; "Impossible Reasons for Housekeeping"; "Like Mirabai"; "House of Mist"; "Running Man"

My special gratitude to Zarina for preparing a woodcut "River and Bridge" specially for this book of poems.

Contents

I. BLOOD LINE

Relocation 3
Softly My Soul 4
Everything Strikes Loose 5
South of the Nilgiris 6
Passion 8
River and Bridge 12
Toxic Petals 13
Blood Line 14
Palpable Elysium 16
Moving World 17
Skin Song 18
Muse 23
Muse (2) 24

II. NEWS OF THE WORLD

News of the World 27
Lost Language 29
City Street 31
Brown Skin, What Mask? 33
Against Elegy 34
Art of Pariahs 35
The Young of Tiananmen 36
Prison Cell 37
For Safdar Hashmi 39
Moloyashree 41
Paper Filled with Light 42
Desert Rose 44
Estrangement Becomes the Mark of the Eagle 45
Asylum 47
No Man's Land 49

III. MANDALA

Room without Walls 53
Landscape with Door 54
Sweet Water 55
Elephants in Heat 56
Mandala 58
The Unexceptional Drift of Things 60
Generation 61
Under the Incense Tree 63
Ashtamudi Lake 65
No Witnesses 71
Impossible Reasons for Housekeeping 72
Like Mirabai 73
House of Mist 74

IV. SAN ANDREAS FAULT

Running Man 77
Revelation 77
High Noon 78
Raw Bird of Youth 79
Indian Sandstone 80
Sweet Alyssum 81
San Andreas Fault 83
Deer Park at Sarnath 88

I.
BLOOD LINE

Relocation

Scraping it all back:

A species of composition
routine as crossing streets
or taking out the garbage
nothing to blow the mind

Done over and over in the light
of small events, a street
with shining windows where a man
on a ladder hangs in the wind

As Broadway thickens with bicycles,
intrepid walkers rise up to the sun,
and brittle magnolias lift petals
from abandoned traffic islands.

The road to the hospital
is contagious already, the trees
taut, argentine. Picked clean by winter
they make icons of our difficulty:

The mind held in a metallic fork—
its sense inviolate, the questions of
travel scored by icy borders,
the imagination ordering itself.

Softly My Soul

Softly my soul, softly O so softly
the horses are gone, the elephants too, hooves pittering
the sky is pink, the water suffused with leaves

The west is harsh, the east too, the last airplane
flashes on the horizon, the herons are pink
brushing the skies. Someone in the plane cries out

Hoarse gutturals, no sweetness there: "Immigrants
where you begin, name each common thing
grass blade, sappy stalk, weeds scratching clouds

Disorder under the bridge—the poor man's head
bent into a trashcan, the rich in white cadillacs
tigers in your dreams, wildebeest moaning

And all the fragrant disorder of garments
shredded, packed into knapsacks, hoisted
against a shoulder blade bloodied with old burdens."

Softly my soul, softly O so softly
the herons have fled, but the planes keep coming.
Above Liberty's torch the sky is pink

And George Washington would laugh in his sleep
to mark the gazelles on Fifth Avenue
tiny miniskirts hoisted to their thighs

Now a voice on the airport intercom cries:
"I might be a car salesman, a truck driver
a packer of crimson tomatoes and plums

"A washer of dishes, a peddlar of T shirts.
Or must I stand here and wait in midseason
till some excellence comes in search of me?"

Softly my soul, softly O so softly
there is something invisible you must press through
the asphalt shimmering with scales is indigo.

Everything Strikes Loose

In the end
everything strikes loose

Look at my hands
that held you
as the pepper vines
hold to the mango tree
my child, my first child

What fuels the mind
I tell myself
is not grief,
not waste:
just a bird beak
scuffing up leaves
at the tree's base.

Yet see
the pepper vines slip,
roots clustering
colorless as air.

I plucked the first
fruits for you,
the sour stuff
you spat, the sweet
dribbled down your chin.

You were greedy then
"Amma!" you cried, pointing

I could not see
if the blackness
at the pepper's core
had burnt you.

The glare
was in my eyes,
the flickering leaves,
the golden Pamba river.

Now the river trickles
through low hills,
it tastes of childhood

The boats fly no flags
the races are all done
and flat barges driven by men
bear cinnamon, cloves, dried pepper.

South of the Nilgiris

My son who is young
just six this year
knows the red soil of our land

Turning it in his palm
he said
"My sister is this earth
I am water
we will mix together."

I heard this in a dream

He pointed at my belly
watermelon swollen
streaked as if mud
had dribbled over
lighter flesh

"I am glad
I was not born a girl.
I will never hold that weight
in my belly."

He spun on his heels,
on his lean shoulders
I saw wings of bone
pale as the stones of Kozhencheri

"Mother!" he laughed
"You know I am not a girl!"

Under my ribs
she turned
his unborn sister,
green as a wave
on the southern coast
ready to overwhelm me,
overwhelm even the distant hills.

Passion

I.

After childbirth
the tenth month's passion:

a bloodiness
still shifting at her core
she crawls on the mud floor

past the empty rice sacks
blown large with dust,
rims distended like sails.

Her skin scrapes a tin bowl
with water from the stream,
a metal frame

bearing a god
whose black blue face
melts into darkness, as a gem might

tossed back
into its own
implacable element.

She waits,
she sets her sari to her teeth
and when the chattering begins

fierce, inhuman joy,
monkeys rattling the jamun tree,
bellies distended, washed with wind

she screams
and screams
a raw, ungoverned thing.

II.

There are beetles scrabbling
in the open sacks,
chaff flies in the half light
a savage sound in her eyes
struck free

the human realms of do and don't
the seemingly precise, unalterable keys
dashed to a frenzy
and still the voice holds.

III.

One summer's day
I saw a heron
small and grey
blinded by an eagle's claw

it dashed its head
against the Coromandel rock.

The bleeding head
hung on
by a sinew or two
as the maimed bird
struck
and struck again
then turned to rise
an instant
on its sunlit wings.

It was carved in bronze
against the crawling foam

agony
the dead cannot know
in their unaltered kingdoms.

IV.

I am she
the woman after giving birth

life
to give life
torn and hovering

as bloodied fluids
baste the weakened flesh.

For her
there are no words,
no bronze, no summoning.

I am her sight
her hearing
and her tongue.

I am she
smeared with ash
from the black god's altar

I am
the sting of love
the blood hot flute
the face
carved in the window,
watching as the god set sail

across the waters
risen from the Cape,
Sri Krishna in a painted catamaran.

I am she
tongueless in rhapsody

the stars of glass
nailed to the Southern sky.

Ai ai

she cried.

They stuffed
her mouth with rags

and pulled her
from the wooden bed

and thrust her
to the broken floor.

I,   I.

River and Bridge

Trees on the other side of the river
so blue, discarding light into water, a flat
white oil tank with HESS in black, a bridge
Holzer might skim with lights—*I will take her
down before she feels the fear*—no sarcophagus here:

I have come to the Hudson's edge to begin my life
to be born again, to seep as water might
in a landscape of mist, burnished trees,
a bridge that seizes crossing.

But Homer knew it and Vyasa too, black river
and bridge summon those whose stinging eyes
crisscross red lights, metal implements,
battlefields: birth is always bloody.

Toxic Petals

From where I sit
summer's blossoms are headless
tearing uphill

Trees tossed in weeds
swivel the sky
to a blue hole.
It sucks up my reflection

I have no face,
my skin is a net
stretched to rock

Where the river
pounds so dark
it is more than memory

And the warrior, my cousin
wades right in.

Light swarms
to his cut knee,
his eyes are not wasted
with killing.

He bears me
in his arms

I am black,
featureless
chockfull of poems

Toxic petals
torn from the landscape
buzz and snarl in me

I share his arms.
I am a goddess now
four armed and skinless

None of us
is cut in gold.
I feel the cold come on.

Blood Line

For Svati Mariam, one year old

My child is rain
on the tamarind tree

She is an enemy
to burnt grass,
to fruit sieved
with metal

Struck
from a stunted branch.

She is my mother's
mother who cries in me,
my line of blood
our perpetuity.

When wild deer
track the mud
for buried roots

I'll grip my blouse
and loosen it

I'll show her how
my throat can hang
a woman's weight.

In the sky's bowl
after a season of storm
we'll watch girls
with antlers in their hair

Dance, confounding
ancient hunters
who stumble westward
broken bows in hand.

Palpable Elysium

Ten years later still stranger here
I hunch by a forked stump set into soil.
Will it pitch, pour into bloom at springtime?

Can my hands set right simple things?
Forsythia, mountain laurel, petals stitched in pink,
black flowering cherry, a foreign strain
as the man at Callender's explained

Grafted to local root
it takes to the broken slate
the somewhat alkaline soil of the Hudson valley.

Pondering this so silently, I peer into the hole
where grass burnt last summer.
A shadow crawls.

I glimpse a hawk
brown spanned thing, crude,
bearing its own death in its wings.

A child with a shovel in her hand
raising clumps of clay,
tight red boots flashing on the hill.

Moving World

For Adam Kuruvilla

To be at home
everywhere in the late world
as the Buddha taught:

I ponder this as
waterlilies spawn fragrances
in a pond filled with waste

Muskrats nibble on bent
stalks pumice colored,
ravenous with sap

My fourteen-year-old child
deepvoiced, muscular
loiters in the light

Aslant on a basketball field
close to a highway
where trailers crawl:

They are stacked with tents
folding chairs, drums for
strange festivals—

To be at home everywhere
in this moving world,
as the Buddha taught.

Skin Song

Within the heart a mirror but no face shows
You'll see the face when the heart's doubleness goes.
                              KABIR

Perceives that the corpse is slowly borne from the eating and sleeping rooms of the house . . .
                            WHITMAN

I.

Time was a drift of wing, claw, vine
petal, stalk, skin of my tongue, wrapping up
stones so sweet to suck. I skipped through dirt and muck
the short streams singing,
green scales dropped from my eyes
glittering in pieces.

I cannot spell it out
but when the hearse with black painted wheels
skirted the dirt, the bamboo grove hissed
the banana trees curtsied in heat, in terrible heat
I hid in a room.
On tiptoe I peered, throat between bars.

Water they had drawn for his last bath
sheened the mahogany.
Laid out naked his dear dark body
indigo globes of eyes, nostrils cast in bone
feet arced, soles flecked with calluses.

II.

When the iron wheels on the hearse
cut into dirt and men dressed in white
sweat in their eyes strode by the wheels of the hearse
when the silvery groin of bamboo and lime
shimmered in dirt

Tongue thick with soil I roared, I belched my grief.
I was a catch in God's throat, a giggle, a gut gripe
I was vermillion threaded into rice paper
sheathe of sun and moon
time's masquerade

Slit in the vulva as the head
of the too-big-child tore the mother's tender skin.
I was speech swallowing death,
verbs all shame stanched: *Vak Vak, Vak*
crouching, shitting, guts cramped in childbirth
the wide shouldered bull headed child
butting the mother-to-be.
She squats astride a blackness monstrous, driven deep
through lips that will not sleep.

"Amma Ila, amma," whispers a girl child
licking a skein of dirt that drops from a mango tree.
It babbles on her tongue weave of silk, wood, dung
love's calumny.
She will not go to grandfather's funeral
watch his dear dark body shovelled into dirt.
Indoors she digs knuckles into eyes
rubs her face to the sky; does not cry.

III.

Now everything is hurt and harm
pebbles on a beach where water slops,
bold stripes on a child's skirt
a whip, a stripped cadence for a sun
that slits pink clouds to threads

She strolls on the beach
two children clinging to her
she sees very little,
by the water's edge over mounds of stone
waves flap, plastic shreds dance their rotting.
White sails are pasted to the horizon.

IV.

Time was a lyric did not sting
and a cloud cover over the kitchen wall
was streaked in gold,
but how grim it was under the crow's throat
the child stuffing herself with sweets
as rain slashed pillowcases,
delicate muslins in the window sills.

In the kitchen under the rinsed blade
blood ran down the drain into the hill.

There was blood on her skirt
it was as her mother feared
it was not the juice of the black jamun
she rolled on her tongue, crushed in her gums
nor the overripe guava she spat at the sun
nor dribbled flesh of the watermelon.

With the pad between her legs
she could not walk very well

waddled at first, sidled as best she could
she learnt to wash out stains in cold water
with a bit of salt flung in.
She felt sore and shamed fresh and burnt.

Child of the soft mouth
the wordless part, remember me.

V.

Time was a python new killed
dripped its black stuff onto a dirt road
where the hearse stuck, wheels trapped in stones
elephants loitering in a temple processional
some hours earlier had loosed.

Time was the gap in the bars through which she peered
barefoot, squarejawed.
She thrust her head towards the shower of light
from the gooseberry tree
glimpsed games marked on hands and knees

Grandfather and she playing at Ashoka's elephants
round and round the bed of tiger lilies
or peering through a bush, one eye shut on one face
to make up Shiva's three.

They took turns at that, it was a good game
"Shabash" he clapped, his gaunt hand
with knuckles cramped
like wildfowl perched in the kitchen eaves,
crouched tight over beams, broken tiles
swept with sunlight scraped from gooseberries,
musky fruit fuzz, stiff caramel colored stalks
that cannot yield to mouth or palm
stinting eternity

Stuck like a hearse glimpsed
in the far corners of a picture
someone else has made with white robed men
dragging the cart from church
dirt blowing in swirls, a horizon
of bamboo flat and dry as glue.

VI.

Time was a drift of wing, claw, vine
petal, stalk, skin of her tongue,
skin of a python struck with poles, eyes mashed
where the men made a ring and beat and beat
scales tough, corrosive, making iron glints

Making a sky, a theater of words that rotate and pound
the horizon a scene doubling itself
sheer as rice paper shielding sun and moon
heart's catastrophe in an unequal play
no hand could ever script.

She stops, she loosens all her clothes
she strips herself of silks, cottons,
bangles, necklaces, pins, slips off her rings.

She kneels to touch
the molten stuff from the python's head
then open eyed, she steps into the gutted skin
dances on a bloodied thing
mirroring paradise.

Muse

She walks towards me, whispering
Dried petals in her hair
A form of fire

But her skin,
like finest Dacca cotton
drawn through a gold ring, spills

Over bristling water.
Something has hurt her.
Can a circlet of syllables

Summon her from the Vagai river?
She kneels by a bald stone
cuts glyphs on its side, waves to me.

Our language is in ruins—
vowels impossibly sharp,
broken consonants of bone.

She has no home.

Why gossip about her
shamelessly—you household gods,
raucous, impenitent ?

Muse (2)

"Our language is in ruins.
No—not Something," she whispers to me
 "not About or Here.
It's a doing thing that spurns me

"The prams are filled with ash.
These are my syllables.
Can you understand that?"

Furious now, red sari whirling,
she's naked by the Vagai river.
But no one cares, neither washermen
nor moist buffaloes.

"Creatures of Here and There
we keep scurrying
Madurai, Manhattan, who cares?"

When she turns it is etched on her:
words, sentences, maps,
her skin burns bright:

Sheer aftermath.

II.
NEWS OF THE WORLD

News of the World

We must always return
to poems for news of the world
or perish for the lack

Strip it
block it with blood
the page is not enough
unless the sun rises in it

Old doctor Willi writes
crouched on a stoop
in Paterson, New Jersey.

I am torn by light

She cries into her own head.
The playing fields of death
are far from me. In Cambodia I carried
my mother's head in a sack
and ran three days and nights
through a rice field

Now I pick up vegetables
from old sacking and straighten
them on crates: tomatoes
burning plums, cabbages hard
as bone. I work in Manhattan.

The subway corrupts me
with scents the robed Muslims sell
with white magazines
with spittle and gum

I get lost underground

By Yankee Stadium
I stumble out

hands loaded down
fists clenched into balls

A man approaches
muck on his shirt
his head, a battering ram
he knows who I am

I stall :
the tracks flash
with a thousand suns.

Lost Language

It comes in flight
towards me
brushing against
an old stone wall
father's father raised

Language so fine
it cannot hold the light
for long and beats
as water might

Inside my quiet room
the reckonings of autumn
come clear—

The wellside where she
labored in the wind,
a blindness in her eyes
striking as water might

The earthen pot
mounds of bloodied cloth
a granite block
she dashed the clothes against
then scrubbed them taut

Gunfire on the hill
grenades in a lotus pond
guava leaves torn
muddied by the mill
where water turns

And poems with chill
syllables cluster
like migrant storks
all tender and tense

Their routes invisible
to me—I crouch
in the white silks
I wore when I met you

Dumb with tenderness
that stirs stone wall
and feverish hill.

City Street

A table on a rooftop
stripped by frost

Who set it there?
Is this mere description?

My two hands pour
from a high window

They make a flag to the nations
They are crying in the street

There is no bread on the table
filled with cold,
no milk, no rice, no water.

No sickle there, nor hammer.

*

It is as if I had died
as if we all had died

Not of hunger or thirst,
just turned

The sheer fact of the matter
gives us pause

As a burnt dosa on a griddle
as idlis wasting in steam.

And having gone
cried out for resurrection.

*

The angelic orders
do not haunt us any longer

The trees are not bent
to human shape: thigh, wrist, vulva.

We cannot cry: "Who will hear us now?"
Not that we lack voices or breath.

On this city street
the clash of small arms bought second hand

In rain, in heat
prevents us

The sexual flash diminished,
blunt missiles loaded by children.

Or a stench
very like flesh

A fingertip caught on the rack
when food was set in the oven.

***

Listen, the trees are cut in iron.
This is my poem.

Brown Skin, What Mask?

Babel's township seeps into Central Park
I hunch on a stone bench scraping nightingale-bulbuls
 cuckoo-koels, rose-gulabs off my face

No flim-flam now; cardsharp, streetwise
I fix my heels at Paul's Shoe Place for a dollar fifty
get a free make-over at Macy's, eyes smart, lips shine.
Shall I be a hyphenated thing, Macaulay's Minutes
and Melting Pot theories notwithstanding?

Shall I bruise my skin, burn up into
She Who Is No Color whose longing is a crush
of larks shivering without sound?

When lit by his touch in a public place
—an elevator with a metal face—shall I finger grief for luck
work stares into the "bride is never naked" stuff?

Against Elegy

Sick to death of elegies
where she swooned her flesh away
sick to death of the Ubi Sunt Variations
ou sont les neiges etc.

She selected hotshot hockey players
with elegant thigh muscles
clean shaven quarterbacks in damp shirts
for her boogie-woogie dance in sneakers and top hat
and G-string made of a silken thing she tore
from a six-yard Kancheepuram sari

At the West End Bar to catcalls, sodden roars,
heavy bellied, flushed, tin trident hurting her chin
she pranced :"Blood rings its own Thing"
she sang in honor of Shiva.

Art of Pariahs

Back against the kitchen stove
Draupadi sings:

In my head Beirut still burns

The Queen of Nubia, of God's Upper Kingdom
the Rani of Jhansi, transfigured, raising her sword
are players too. They have entered with me
into North America and share these walls.

We make up an art of pariahs:

Two black children spray painted white
their eyes burning,
a white child raped in a car
for her pale skin's sake,
an Indian child stoned by a bus shelter,
they thought her white in twilight.

Someone is knocking and knocking
but Draupadi will not let him in.
She squats by the stove and sings:

The Rani shall not sheathe her sword
nor Nubia's queen restrain her elephants
till tongues of fire wrap a tender blue,
a second skin, a solace to our children

Come walk with me towards a broken wall
—Beirut still burns—carved into its face.
Outcastes all let's conjure honey scraped from stones,
an underground railroad stacked with rainbow skin,
Manhattan's mixed rivers rising.

The Young of Tiananmen

If I had crimson I would write with it
for the battle of Tiananmen
raise garlands of orchids, roses
blood-sucking Venus Trap flowers

For the young with black silken hair
unstrapping fear from their thighs
raising it aloft like a banner, singing
"China, newborn China, be our shield."

If I had indigo I would write with it
for the battle of Tiananmen
raise garlands of hooks, eyes,
burst bone, torn cartilage
mucus that shines with death

For the young with black silken hair
unstrapping fear from their thighs
raising it aloft like a banner singing
"China, newborn China, be our shield."

But old men with glue in their
bones, wax in their hip sockets
flesh in their teeth cracked
sticks, whips, ropes with rusty nails

Tanks rolled, guns coughed
tear gas choked them in pitiful
sobs: the young of Tiananmen.
From a far country I sing

As blood swallowed them whole
they became our blood
as the sun swallowed them whole
they became children of the sun

What ink can inscribe them now
the young of Tiananmen?

Prison Cell

The season is clear, hot
everything magnified
in that cell where you squat
even an ant, a fly
would be company

Open eyed you watch
the jailor dash
a mess of beans, gruel
onto an upturned bucket

Who is this man
this brutal guardian?
An ordinary sting from wasp
or fly would hurt him too?
You wonder.

Later that night
wide awake you tremble.
Pressing through walls
and iron grille
the souls that compose you
enter in

Massed, magisterial
spirits of the dead, lordly
moving slow over manacles
and scrap metal,
township, field and hill

The living too
half grown girls, youths, men, women
little ones crying as they do
for little things
torment you

A ball, a broken hoop
a crust of bread ground up
mixed with water

You push your palms
into the shining stuff
the night is clear, everything magnified

You clench your fists
and draw it in,
ferocious power, speechless, still

Till your woman's flesh
poised against the wall
resembles a statued thing

Lord of oath and redemption
cut from mahogany, marked all over
with screws, wires, chains, razor bits.

NOTE: This poem was completed on June 18, 1990 and read out that night at the ceremony "Words of Praise for the Mandelas and the ANC" held at the New School for Social Research, New York City.

For Safdar Hashmi Beaten to Death Just Outside Delhi

Safdar it is done:

A courtyard with four walls
where the lock did not hold
a faulty pump, water trickling
out of sight

A winter's day in Jhandapur
under these leaves
wet with light
death a player hundred armed

Clubbed and ringed:
how tight you held the door
so others might race
over wall and stony field

I hear you now knocking
at my door seeking entry.
This room is framed by trees
stones, walls, bare sky

So blue it might be Delhi
in winter all over again
and by the open window
your half finished play

The actors drenched
in black repeating it
to stubborn stones
children crouched by walls

Grown men and women
packed by the factory walls
and in the distance
the hodge-podge of state

Trucks, tanks, a convoy
of arms irregular, ill-sorted
with boy soldiers, hundred
headed, breathing hard.

NOTE: Safdar Hashmi, a young Marxist playwright, was beaten to death on January 1, 1989 while performing the play *Halla Bol* in support of the rights of striking workers. Two days after his death, the players of the Jan Natya Manch (including his wife Moloyashree) returned to the very spot and completed the play.

Moloyashree

Moloyashree
you come to me in fine weather—

An old mattress with pin pricks
in it puffs cotton;
I see stones and sticks
a child skips over
a woman beats a pan
scraping out burnt milk
stoops behind a torn curtain
crying "Ram, Sri Ram, Ram"
crickets flash in mounds of wheat.

Already the sun's in your teeth
the bizarre ivory it turns of a Delhi winter
so fierce it stings cloth and hair.

There
     there they beat him by the tap
on scalp and skull with bits of rock
lathis tipped with steel, wrought iron
broken from the construction site.

You point out the spot, so silently
drawing your palms apart as if your
soul and his still hung on a thread

So hot only the dead could work
that needle, crawl through its eye.

Paper Filled with Light

In memory of Uma Shankar Joshi (1911–1989)

I.

Under a plum tree a stone that weeps water
under a roof of wood, paper filled with light
Noguchi understood this emptiness, this discipline
his father's blackening heart he turned to sheer stone

A circlet for our hands titled Sun at Midnight
or Spirit's Flight, cool torsion cut to Carrara marble

I whisper these things to you as I stand in Isamu's garden
in cool September, under a plum tree, wanting to add
in my usual way—here, in another country—as if
the germ of death were on my tongue already

But there's no distance between us now; you who lived
by the word are wholly immortal, your lines burnt into history.

II.

Under a plum tree, a stone that weeps water
in Setu, under a roof of wood, paper filled with light

You clarified this discipline, seizing emptiness
the precise weights of the palpable
fired by the fury of sight, speech arced to the extremities
of the known, fronting the axe of displacement:

The massacres of '47, the killing fields of Partition,
Gandhi, his eyes burnt into prayers—He fasted,
we all did in those days, fasting for peace—
In '84 in Trilokpuri a girl child raped, stabbed in the riots,

Her mother bent over a cooking pot trembling,

mouth stuffed with stones. Poetry as witness:
silk torn so the blackness of the frame can remember
the limbs the bloodied stuff that makes us a nation.

III.

Above the plum tree this northern sky is streaked with pink almost
as if we were in Gandhi's ashram
by rocks with mouths ruder than plumstones
by water so empty it takes color from the sky

In the dry season before the river splintered
before you pitched yourself into a dream so steep
your daughters could not clamber down the edge
to hook father's syllables from whorled water, blackest ink.

IV.

Uma Shankar I ask you now, what is the sun at midnight?
The spirit's flight? The gold roof of heaven?

What is death doing in the throats of those
from your Bamna, my Tiruvella crouched in Jordan's deserts?

What is death scribbling on their cheeks
as they stumble to a water truck long run dry?

I am here in Isamu's garden, by an old warehouse,
by a children's park, by the East River—rusty gasoline tanks, the
packed cars of new immigrants, the barbed wires
of Meerut, Bensonhurst, Baghdad, strung in my brain.

How could I sing of a plum tree, a stone that weeps water?
How could I dream of paper filled with light?

(8 – 18 September, 1990)

Desert Rose

All the seven skies
are broken
a bright wind seals
the infant's mouth

Sand dunes reap
the pillaged city
the vine bears
fruit

Colossal grapes
of rock
black rock
to have

Or hold
at heart
the driven self
near sightless

As hands
split bread
and strip
the desert rose.

Estrangement Becomes the Mark of the Eagle

I.

We lie in a white room, on a bed with many pillows
next to a window just above a street
You whisper: exile is hard
let me into your mouth, let me blossom

I listen for I know the desert is all around
the muggers and looters, caravan men with masked faces
and Mesopotamia's largesse under tanks
and the colonels of Texas and Florida
with cockatoo feathers in their caps
and the young lads of Oregon torn from their pillows
bent under bombs, grenades, gas masks
and the young lads of Kuwait beheaded in the sand.

II.

Estrangement becomes the mark of the eagle
a signal corpus, bonanza of dew
the portals of paradise are sunk

Yet all that surrenders as we do, lover infant godhead,
nothing makes blank, nothing kills, not
the chill hauteur of elegies, not gunshot wounds
But vision clamps. Bloodied feathers
in a young woman's mouth, torn from a colonel's cap,
she spits them out, she comes from Tiruvella, my hometown
heart under cover, belly huge in desert sand she squats
by the barbed wire of a transit camp outside Amman

Behind her back a ziggurat of neon
marking the eagle's pure ascent
in whose aftermath small bodies puff with ash.

III.

We lie in a white room, on a bed with many pillows
just above the street, the world's a blackened market place

No codicil: Mujh-se pahli-si mahabbat . . . dearest heart
I can no longer repeat the rest of that.

Where we are a child, her jeans filled with blood
gags on dropped vegetables, half cooked rice
she picked up as she knelt in the trash.
Below her, smashed subway cars imported from Japan
crumple thirty feet down underneath our gate

While men well trained to the purchase of power
knot water bottles, burst cans of shaving cream
spent condoms, to the rear ends of jeeps and race
at the crack of dawn, at the bitten end of our century
through Broadway, through narrow desert tracks.

NOTE: The entire line runs: *Mujh-se pahli-si mahabbat, meri mahbub, na mang*. It is the first line of the celebrated poem by Faiz Ahmed Faiz and in translation may be rendered as : "Beloved, do not ask me for that love again."

Asylum

Late at night, on a bed with many pillows
next to a window, high above a street
you read to me: the gutturals of your mother
tongue rough with desire, lit by pain
—a poet who must crawl to god's gate—

Cast down before your great gate
I cry out in the darkness for asylum
—No, it is more like shriek, fiercer than cry,
the translator was too soft, didn't get it right—

And you read on, in the language of Qabbani,
Adonis, Darwish, in the syllables of your mother's speech
the deserts of Nejd stir in your brain.
While I, I long to cry in my woman's way

Cover me in your arms we're in Hell's Kitchen
don't you see? There's Yama doped out, vials split by his heels
and Cerberus licking up clots of burnt milk

To come to you, to lie on this bed with many pillows
in a white room, high above a street
I have peeled my thighs off a wall
the skin of my mouth from the insides of a refrigerator.

I think I am a bridge of burning paper.
Love, sweet love, your arms must lower me
thirty feet below this floor
into a harsh desert the translator does not see.

In the sudden heat I'll watch
old men and women, soldiers and civilians crawl
with the ambulances, past fractured traffic lights
chained subway stops, towards the palace door.

Shall God's gate grant asylum?
Badr Shakir al-Sayyab—"I wish to die"
is how you end your poem—do you know?

NOTE: The lines come from the poem "Before the Gate of God" by Badr Shakir al-Sayyab the Iraqi poet. He was born near Basra in 1927 and died in Kuwait in 1964. He was buried on the outskirts of Basra.

No Man's Land

The dogs are amazing
sweaty with light
they race by the dungheaps

Infants crawl
sucking dirt from sticks
whose blunt ends
smack of elder flesh
and ceaseless bloodiness.

The soldiers though
are finally resting
by the river
berets over their noses

Barges from the north
steam past nettles
cut stalks of blackthorn
and elder, olive trees
axed into bits

Women wash their thighs
in bloodied river water
over and over
they wipe their flesh

In stunned
immaculate gestures,
figures massed with light

They do not hear
the men
or dogs or children.

III.
MANDALA

Room without Walls

We enter a house
through a door
and through that
another
ebony knobs twirl
ivories crack
spinning silk crazy

What drenches us
is music so mute
keys glow red
hinges lock
lodged in clouds

It warbles in me:
a room without walls
a blue blanket
a child might have used
your silver ring
tangling my hair

The prose
of my world
unfixed.

Landscape with Door

Was Sankara right?
Is the world a forest on fire?

In the first burn of light
across the room
you watch me climb

The iron rose
turns feverish as you stand
beside these trees that have no provenance

Being neither here nor there
higher than the chalk cliff
where squirrels scratched their claws

Lower than whirlpools
where elephants splashed
in unseasonable weather.

Whole stanzas turn
bewildered, matches held
over torrents of fire.

Your hands
that touched me twice
unpack a square of paper

A child's drawing of a door,
a makeshift house
lacquered in flame.

Sweet Water

In the village where we met
the incense trees grow shorter

Over green hills
clouds at uncertain altitudes
cast shadows, gingerly

A stream
vanishing underground
reappears in stumpy wetlands

Sags into red
river reeds
bruising us both.

In a dream
the gods might cherish
Up and Down, Then and Now
There and Here absolved

You kneel
you knot my sari
to an incense tree
then lower me

Hand over hand
past the balconies of childhood

Grown sisters at twilight
pouring tea
into glass cups
with handles

Uncles in starched dhotis
popping their cigars,
infants dazed with milk.

I skirt
sweet water
your mouth is so dark.

Here the rocks have old names
and the air is not treacherous.

Elephants in Heat

Soon after we met
you sent me a book
it had many pictures of elephants

I saw a male beast
scorched by stove fire
belly and curling tail stacked
with precise flesh
eyes irregular in passion.

On the margins faced in red,
two others sporting,
a female down below
licked by waterlilies,
buoyant in the curlicues of waves.

I used to make up nightmares as a child
so mother would come in
and lift me up, lips wet
in all that moonlight.

I saw elephants in heat
crawl over garden trees
the myna's nest slipped loose,
it clung to ivory

The sky was colored in blood
as in this painting
Elephant on a Summer Day
Bundi School, circa 1750.

I wonder what it knew
that painter's eye
seared by a fullness we cannot seize
in stanzas stone or canvas
short of stark loss

Our wiry bounding lines
silks and weathered ivories
scored by the Kerala sun

Thinned and dissolved
into desire's rondures
mad covenant of flesh

A beast unpacking
delight from his trunk
your tongue scorching mine
under cover this spring season

As sulphur bubbles from limestone
and the unquiet heart
like the pale monkey in the painting
takes it all in.

Mandala

I can see you now: behind your head a hole
where a bird flies in, flame in its beak
all cut in silk from the robes of a Chinese emperor.

At his death the silks were borne
over the mountains to Tibet, parti-colored threads
stitched into the borders of blessedness.

Our city is all glass: trees, streets, horses
with ice in their manes dragging open carts
glass towers in fractions.

The Tibetan tanka rests on a dealer's wall
on a side street off Madison Avenue.
On it a bird of paradise with no name
except that, a calling which in darkness cries out

Pomegranate streaked wings dragged to the right
against corn colored silks, a stiffness
of bird flesh swallowing its own shadow.

Closer at hand
in the Museum of Natural History
the Kalachakra Mandala shivers under arc lights.

You have taught me this:
the figuration of blessedness is never tranquil,
it is singular not to be cast away.
Later for us that very day, sunlight, shame

Your pipes all seven of them laid
in a semicircle beside a mirror;
in a book you had, a stele with flying figure
female, Indic in origin
palms clasped to a beloved throat;
bedclothes in a heap
toothbrush on the floor

spurts of smoke drifting to a high window
no wings visible.

The city locks us both into a hole:
the past's a scratch
against the density of framed silks,
a seizure in the heart.

This yearning almost spends me—
harsh, impenitent, naming names and streets
and meeting places no one we live with will ever know

Ourselves a crooked hieroglyph,
two wings snapped into a sail
as time scrapes itself together
in fiery, stunted waves.

I stand at the window
as sunlight crushes glass into a rose
and men in turbulent rings,
not gods but as gods might be, tousled, muscular
punch ears and bloody nose and leap
over the wall at Central Park South

Into the spew of cars, fast hooves,
the asphalt of a road bordered by winter trees,
black river almost

Love's trajectory
where a silken thing centuries old
flies in courting death, and natural histories
cast into skin, nipple and nail

Prevail, solving time's compassion.

NOTE: The Kalachakra Mandala (Wheel of Time Mandala), a figuration for the Blessing of Time, was created by Tibetan Monks in the Museum of Natural History, New York City. The entire intricate surface was formed by the patient pouring out of multicolored sands. It was the first time that this sacred form was created outside Tibet. Upon its completion the sands were poured away.

The Unexceptional Drift of Things

What alters in me, alters
everything
        print of elderberries in a dentist's room,
gold spires on an invisible skyscraper,
a desiccated place where a pond was.

"Haarlem Meer's dried out, flat as a pin,"
your voice on the phone transfixes inches, miles,
fragile things:
        the child in a dream,
helpless in traffic on Broadway,
a horse with a broken hoof, a man as old as you
wrapped in blue, eyes shut tight in a bus shelter

A Roman road in a sixth century map,
four feet long in the museum,
from Sicily to Sri Lanka,
earth flattened into a treadable harmony
                      hell at its heart
Eve and Adam cast out,
crouching in Central Park
her hand wedged in a rock,
then searching out root, stone, sky
                his trembling above hers.

"Three months ago, we walked
and there was water, you wore bright blue."
Suddenly you fall silent
no words to set to gashed gold metal,

slit skins of elderberries, a child's stroller
glistening through rushes in a sun bleached space.

What's fallen's eased
surely those first lovers sensed it too
scrambling to hide their shining nakedness

Male and female finally afloat
in the unexceptional drift of things.

Generation

It is almost winter now:

A broken window
across one hundred and thirteenth street
displays a bouquet of dried flowers

Beneath it
a whitened bowl

A tribute
set by hands
I have never seen

Once we had a high windowed house,
peeling porticoes of longing,
each other glimpsed after sleep
in a gold rimmed mirror

Hand on hand
perfectly composed
in a parti-coloured light
brushed from the mountain slopes

Eclipsing time
whose rightnesses
could perhaps only be misunderstood
for ever after the honeymoon.

*

Now I see you
amidst files and phonecalls,
the ritual haste of office

Nightly returns
as our children clamour
at the door for sticks of love
lumps of care

Binding us
as strong weeds
bind the original herbs
in a rainwashed garden.

Low, swarming low
to the pitch of generation.

Still the mountain we climbed
with its brushwood and tinder
hasn't broken over our heads,
nor splintered the light
in the faces we love.

Nor have we taken leave
of our bodies that fall
into a sap stinging and sweet,
as of autumn
unbearably thickened.

*

Out of the crusted skin
of parturition
our coupled hands must raise
a table wiped free of bitterness
set for the morning meal
with bread
bowls of milk
slightly blue at the rim

in a room where light falls
from a bunch of herbs
drying on a pin.

Under the Incense Tree

Come, you said to me
read me your poem.

The sky was blue
above the mango grove,
I was distracted by its permanence,
by your hands
smaller almost than mine
as you held a glass of water for me.

We sat on wicker chairs
drawn to a veranda wall,
half facing each other.

Only my words were between us.

Nothing trembled
in the glass or out of it.

*

Before I set out to come here this

morning, you said,
turning towards me

I read the Vedic hymn to Ushas.

There were lines that run
something like this: *O Lord*
As the hunter prepares the wild fowl
for feasting

By stripping it
limb from limb

So you ready us for age.

*

The small birds cry
in the incense tree at night

In the lightning storm
wild fowl mate in the air.

You come down the steps
into my mother's garden.
The soil is dark and old.

I pluck the incense fruit for you.

It is hard and green
it is wooden to the touch

Bitten,
it sticks to the teeth.

Until it's burnt
it has no scent

It has no scent of death.

Ashtamudi Lake

I.

Approaching you
I skirmish with disaster

Bridges flee from me:
the spun steel of Brooklyn
Manhattan's avenues of metal

I am speeding over
Ashtamudi Lake

Where the train toppled in
where girls in white
a whole year later
tossed flowers

In a death ceremony
for corpses unshriven
swarming in water

If someone sings
an elegy
I do not hear it.

II.

In the carriage
I read a sign in Hindi first
Aag then in English
Prevent Fire

At Kayankulam the fish plates
lie in a stack
worn doors ripped
massed in a shining heap

Dragged from underwater
carriages rust
on their sides
immense as poor houses

Innards beaten out
with chisel and hammer.

III.

Twelve years ago
I fled a mirrored room

Money plants on the sill
an Englishman's love seat
and four-poster complete
with striped furbelows—
Percy's Hotel, Secunderabad.

Earlier that day
across a table crushed
with friends I glimpsed you
for the first time

I set my hand in yours
I followed you
into your room

But as you stood
against the bed
I fled, confused, stricken

I could not trust
a thing so molten.

IV.

Now a hot rain falls:
our histories are hinged
a wooden post, a door
into a rambling house,
cracked unfinished architecture

A nation feting itself
on a forty second anniversary
with gunfire on whitewashed colonnades
drumbeats in shore temples
forced marches past prison and penitentiary

Anthems on quarried slopes
where children crouch, picking
stones from rice
under guava trees stooped
with sunlight.

V.

At Kayankulam
in wayside stations,
bus halts where hot tea is sipped
from thick ceramic cups

Quick figures of our past subside:
a portico collapsed
built with cheap concrete—
two children on their way
to school barely escaped

Dust settles on the shrines
for sacred ones
St George with spear and dragon

A goddess with four arms

hands lavish with paint
gripping rubies, lotus, lute
a stack of rupee bills

Billboards for ceramic
toilet bowls lilac and pink
posters for the latest
True Life Movie—a girl

Paper thin, leapt into water
as backdrop to her tiny hands
and face, two men, father and lover
mustachioed, muscular
erect in white dhotis.

Blunted by the processionals
of sight and sound
taxis with loudspeakers advertising
Coconut Oil Shampoo, Tutorial Colleges
that prepare you for Dubai

We forget the hands
of men and women raising
corpses from lakes, stones
for a new highway over
the flooded paddy field

Hands that scoop
ash from cooking fires
lit by the rim of Ashtamudi Lake
with stubble, dried sticks
bloodied gauze thrown out
from the local hospital.

VI.

Nothing stands still:
through the clatter of iron

wheels, wooden shacks, corrugated roofs
whirling by, I cry

What Vasco da Gama saw
in 1498 is fit to burn

Seeking spices and Christians
he came upon this coast
his blunt eyes glimpsed
territories edged with swords
the outposts of conquest.

Out of Europe's pitch heart
her Papal Bulls
the surreal sense of Empire
Henry the Navigator scrawling
on parchment, his compass
packed with steel
came the ships, the menace.

Columbus heading west
dreamt of the Indies
the gentleness of the natives
when he struck earth
appalled him: they greet us with
affection, he wrote, they would
make good slaves; in their ignorance
they pick up swords by the blade
their hands trickle blood.

Arawac or Indian
the names confine
there is nothing for us
in the white man's burden

With shards of sense
fissured, twice born verbs
our history knits itself.

VII.

But who can bear the truth
of her life or his?

Pressed to the barred window
as the train rocks over steel

I think: the cold of Brooklyn
is inconceivable here
yet here too the body's heat
is stored in small things

Jade against the throat
a honey colored freckled fruit
set to the lips, a mark
your ring left on my palm
twelve years ago.

In a glass
in a speeding train
I see your face again
mirrored in mine

Outside is Ashtamudi Lake
on its surface
little is visible:

Fractures of light
a few reeds, floating stubble

The magnets death makes of us all
(the bonus of truth, call it that
if you will), a conquest

Rubbing raw the nervous
interstices of sense

Desire's nuptials lit in us
no elsewhere here

Only a house
held by its own weight
in the mind's space

It's elegant portico
of polished teak
tilting in heat

As we seize a door
with an ivory knob
and come upon flames.

No Witnesses

"When I whispered your name there were no witnesses."

We strolled by a house with a picket fence
towards a forest filled with voices, trees cut into lutes,
pianos, tanpuras warbling water. Downstream your waist
a white sharpness and I was lost, feet fixed in mist,
hair trembling. The buffalo killed with cold
was by me, the bird too, frenzied with falling
whose animal cries were in my throat, that I tried
to mix with the tanpura and lute.
Too much music and the landscape wasted down.

"Later, a beggarwoman with hands smelling of basil
 tied me down with silk ripped from your scarf.
When I whispered your name, no one could see.
The lone sniper was dreaming in a mango tree."

Impossible Reasons for Housekeeping

"Winter in Northfield I felt so weird
bundled up, just eyes and mouth showing
I might have been in purdah," she laughed out loud,
more softly then:"I felt I was not born."
The oddity of things stippled her thoughts

Grains of wheat tied up in tender skins
darkness stacked in stoves, bread burnt raw
mothers in frilled aprons, bustling out of whiteness
hostile, leaving no margin for foreign women,
herding them into grain silos with tiny upright ladders.

Listening to her, he was glad she had returned
to the cafe with the Italian name, on Fourth Street.
He watched her hands move against the cloth
shifting silk irises spiked with jet, pansies
a sheer hot blue, azure surely.

Together, they would brave the slow drag of snow,
impossible reasons for housekeeping,
his dream of rooms risen out of monsoon rain
tables draped in white damask, stained with turmeric
and the acid of dropped vinegar

Desolation in the silken drawing room
his father with cheroot and lacquer spittoon
his grandfather poring over the map of divided India,
coughing on his own bile.

Fastening their arms about each other
they would stave off the loneliness of new immigrants.
He heard her sigh, there was nothing he could say.
Someday they would shed their clothes and fly
plain into the source of winter light
naked, surrendering everything.

Like Mirabai

She picked up pots and pans and kitchen rack
lashed them to her back: the sky was full of stars.

She saw ice float on the river
the houses of New Jersey ghostly, driven by mist
and music from skylights left ajar

Paper thin doors behind picket fences
kitchens where garlic is crushed in innocent palms,
    tongues, livers, hearts astew

In the feverish melancholy of houses,
whose front doors turn red in moonlight
and the slow drone of cars on the overpass.

The longing within her stripped her down so fine
she forgot name, date of birth, ID number
all the finicky parcellings out of fate

And taut demarcations of a fragile zone
fleshly fragrances mingling, a dish of fruit
peaches set amidst pale mango stones

A world too hard to reinvent.
She saw gulls fly inland from the Hudson river
scoring light in the pattern of kitchen knives

"History makes me hoarse!" she cried.
"I'll never set foot in a house again—Like Mirabai!"
And by the river, she set her clattering burden down.

House of Mist

This house is filled with mist.
it pours off branches of the pear tree,
with fruit so large, they seem *musumbi*
thick misshapen fruit, earth's progeny
fit to tumble into soil they hang like stones,
half way to the sky.
                      To come here, I have walked
through heaven's gate:
Swedish Hill sinking through the clouds
a dead child's grave—he jumped into the lake
The English memsahib could not lock her palms
heave the tiny thighs from water.

Now I think I would like to die in this house
mist slipping through the windows
sills wet with it, moistening memory.
                      The mist has absolutely no regard
for the family at breakfast, four dark heads
bent over a platter of cut fruit
quiet teacup, milk jug edged with blue.

But could I live in this house?
That would be a tough call
something too hard to countenance.
But what if a friend
were to step through the curtained doorway?

I see him now, stooped a little in his middle years
hair brushed with mist,
arms awkward, clumsy with dense fruit.
                      At his heels and thighs
raw, bristling with light
scores of cicadas—twanging my name.

IV.
SAN ANDREAS FAULT

Running Man

Late last night a man
in an orange tracksuit
was running over the Parkway by the river

When he got to the middle of the Parkway
he flung out his hands and stood
seized I was sure by recollection.

Such sweetness!
                His arms picked out
by light, cars flashing on the bridge.
That lonely figure, knees
bent, body trembling.

Revelation

The hills are filled
with a cold glare
a trumpet sounds in glass

There is ash on the ash tree
the flimsy cover of nature
is gaudy with blood

Still rustling
leaves pinch themselves
toe loose

What tenderness
was here, just the other day:
what ferocious offerings

Now storks refuse
to cage themselves

to icy routes

And butterflies
surrender their stoniness
to the freight of dreams.

High Noon

(On seeing Edward Hopper's painting at the Whitney)

It is noon. A woman stands
in the doorway of a house.
The house is white, cut by triangular shadow
and the woman, blue dress unbuttoned
stands at the brink of discovery.
Still nothing comes out of her mouth—
I am she, I want to cry
to the thin air of Nyack, Hopper painted on
pale tremulous ground, stiff meadow grass.
The loneliness of living in the flesh
draws us out, half naked, to the edge.
Air crisp with salt, the skies never parting.

Raw Bird of Youth

For Kamala Das

Kamala, what is happening to me?
I lie in bed, scan newsprint for signs of truth:
the OJ Simpson case, car chase and bloodied glove,
a raucous circus stewing in our throats;
derailment by Signal Mountain, the sun flashing umber
on bodies, dropped into the shell of rock;
India's rationalists scorning the faithful—
shall Ganapati, Lord of the open world,
sip milk from tin spoons?
                    Is this all life holds?
Last night in the cab, on Fifth, passing the park,
I heard the raw bird of youth its beak caught in leaves,
scent of petals thickening. Your voice swooping,
settling as you read from "Morning at Apollo Pier":
"Kiss the words to death in my mouth!"
As you spoke the tiles on a roof flashed indigo.
Now, in a speeding cab as red lights clash,
I sense the sudden rush of lilac, mortality's noise.
Kamala, in a brash wilderness, where does love go?

Indian Sandstone

I have kept it apart in the mind
between high hill and halting place
an island one reaches
sometime towards the middle of the journey:
where birds and fishes
stream in incomprehensible light.

Where I enter a room
with a narrow metal bed
a mirror facing a window
where all that is falls
pictureless, abyssal

Till jets of darkness
rough perplexities, prise loose
an ancient likeness brutal and keen
riding memory: a female body
porous stone astride a god

Parvati your left breast so heavy
it aches even in sandstone
your right knee arched to his thigh:
frail symmetry that strikes us
as a conch shell's throat
is struck with whorled remembrances

Sheer aftermath
as if the sea entire
had scudded through in raw persistent waves
as we sat breathing softly
at the edge of the bed, your left hand
holding mine, my fingers
clasped within yours, quiet as Indian sandstone

Mindful of her
whose hands all skin and blood
like ours, reaches night after night,

in hot unsullied dreams for his dear feet
dancing on bloodied elephant hide.

Sweet Alyssum

I.

"I am grateful," she said to me
"for the room a bomb makes when it falls"—she said this sitting
straight under a tree
what tree, I have forgotten now.

She said she was your sister.

I listened to her, burying my head in my hands.
She did likewise.

The olive root from your childhood
its color spent in dreams,
an arrowhead from a bronzed
hillside in Jerusalem
terrible city of the deity
where children pound fists against
rocks colored like cheap plastic balls,

crimson, phosphorus, ivory
the ballast of desire you discovered so early,
casting its own gravity against
the skeletal forms of love we bear within.

"Wen Beitak?" they asked "Nad Evida?"
"Where is your home?"
                        the child battling the fourgated wind
hair blown back, crying into his own eyes
in the schoolyard rough with golden mustard bloom
at the edge of no man's land.

II.

In your dream you came to Ellis Island,
to a humpbacked apple tree
                right where the boats stop,
it stoops over, casting its fruit into black water.
The dream doubled up like a pregnancy
you saw yourself a child again,
at the gates of great Jerusalem.

"He has no home now,
you know that, don't you?"
She said turning towards me,
the woman who claims to be your sister
"As for me, I am grateful
for what I have."

As she moved, digging her heels into rock
I saw the left side of her face
where skin had fused into bone

so deep the burning went

"Maria Nefeli who loves the cloud gatherer"
I whispered
       "or Draupadi born of fire
                    surely you are she
or Demeter even, poised at the bramble pit
where love drove her
or Sita clinging to stone

"Look here is flowering mustard he brought me
from Bethlehem
from the old schoolyard filled
with children, before
                it fell.
                    Sweet alyssum too.
Take it, please."

San Andreas Fault

And if I cried, who'd listen to me in those angelic
orders?   RILKE

I. The Apparition

Too hard to recall each grass blade, burn of cloud
in the monsoon sky, each catamaran's black sail.
Nor very easily, could we make ourselves
whole through supplication,
before and after—the jagged rasp of time,
cooled by winds brushing the Pacific.
The brown heart, rocking, rocking,
ribs dashed to the edge of San Andreas Fault.

Suddenly I saw her, swathed in silk
seemingly weightless, nails prised into rock,
rubber boots dangling over the gorge:

"This morning light over water
drives everything out of mind, don't you agree?
I know the Ganga is like nothing else on earth
but now I fish here.
San Andreas suits me: salmon, seaperch, striped bass."

Montara, Moss Beach, Pescadero, Half Moon Bay,
North American names quiver and flee, pink shrubs,
stalks of the madrone, speckled heather rooting in clumps
and under it all the fault her voice worked free:

"Saw him walking with you, holding hands in sunlight
two of you against a wall: hands, face, eyes, all shining
he had a brown paper bag you nothing. How come?"

Feet hot against madrone roots, veins beating indigo
to the rift where her thighs hung, musically,
unbuckling gravity, I set my face to her squarely:

"Come to America so recently
what would you have me carry in my hands?
In any case why bring in a man I hardly see anymore?"

II. Flat Canvas

Once, waiting for him in the parking lot
right by the tap and muddied pool
where wild dogs congregate
—he was often late—I let the sunlight bathe my face.
Stared into water, saw myself doubled, split
a stick figure, two arms bloodied with a bundle
racing past parked cars of third world immigrants.

Then I saw him sprinting by my side:
"Teeth, Teeth, Teeth,"
he cried his body bolted down, a dream
by Basquiat, flat canvas, three pronged heart, broken skull
laced with spit, skin stretched over a skeleton pierced with nails,
Gray's Anatomy in one hand, in the other, the Bible.

In Malayalam, Hindi, Arabic, French he cried out
turning to English last, babbling as the continental coast
broke free riveting Before and After, jumpstarting reflection.
The Angel of Dread, wings blown back
neck twisted over mounds of rubble
doorposts with blood of the lamb smeared on.
And faintly visible under jarring red
words like "Progress" "Peace" "Brotherly Love"
"One Nation under God" all that stuff.

III: Funeral Song

I sensed his breath on my neck
he needed to suck me into eternity
press thumbs against my throat, set a paper bag

against my thighs, warm with the hot dog he got on the cheap from
the corner store by the supermarket wall.
"A real American hot dog, sauerkraut and all," he boasted
till tears took hold.

He pressed me tight against a tree,
in full sight of an Indian family
struggling with their groceries, thrusting
harder as breath came in spurts—
a funeral song he learnt from his mother
the words from Aswan filling me:

"You have crossed a border, never to return.
Stranger in this soil, who will grant you burial?
Neck of my beloved, who will grant you burial?
Eyes, lips, nose who will shield you from sight?"

Tighter and tighter he squashed me
till the fruits of the fig tree broke loose
and fit to faint I thrust my fist
through his blue cotton shirt, cast myself free.

IV. Package of Dreams

Late at night in Half Moon Bay
hair loosed to the glow of traffic lights
I slit the moist package of my dreams.

Female still, quite metamorphic
I flowed into Kali ivory tongued, skulls nippling my breasts
Durga lips etched with wires astride an electric tiger
Draupadi born of flame betrayed by five brothers stripped
of silks in the banquet hall of shame.

In the ghostly light of those women's eyes
I saw the death camps at our century's end

A woman in Sarajevo shot to death

as she stood pleading for a pot of milk,
a scrap of bread, her red scarf swollen
with lead hung in a cherry tree.

Turks burnt alive in the new Germany,
a grandmother and two girls
cheeks puffed with smoke
as they slept in striped blankets
bought new to keep out the cold.

A man and his wife in Omdurman
locked to a starving child, the bone's right
to have and hold never to be denied,
hunger stamping the light.

In Ayodhya, in Ram's golden name
hundreds hacked to death, the domes
of Babri Masjid quivering as massacres begin—
the rivers of India rise mountainous,
white veils of the dead, dhotis, kurtas, saris,
slippery with spray, eased from their bloodiness.

V. San Andreas Fault

Shaking when I stopped I caught myself short
firmly faced her: "What forgiveness here?"
"None," she replied "Every angel knows this.
The damage will not cease and this sweet gorge
by which you stand bears witness.

"Become like me a creature of this fault."

She said this gently, swinging to my side
body blown to the fig tree's root.

"Stop," I cried, "What of this burden?
The messy shroud I stepped into?
Ghostly light? Senseless mutilations?"

Her voice worked in my inner ear
sorrow of threshed rice,
cadences of my mother tongue loosed in me:

"Consider the glory of the salmon
as it leaps spray to its own death,
spawn sheltered in stone under running water.
That's how we make love—Can you understand?
Each driven thing stripping itself
to the resinous song of egg and sap
in chill water.

"Sometimes I think this is my mother's country
she conceived me here, legs splayed, smoke in her eyes
in the hot season when gold
melts from chains, beads, teeth
and even the ceremonials of the dead
dwelt on in Upper Egypt, dissolve away.

"We are new creatures here.
Hooking fish in San Andreas we return them to the fault
perch, black salmon, the lot.

"When the walls of your rented room
in Half Moon Bay fall away
consider yourself blessed.

"The snows of the Himalayas
glimpsed in your mother's songs
once came from rainclouds high above this coast
cradling the rafters of the seven heavens."

Deer Park at Sarnath

It seems impossible to begin
to speak of those gone ahead
intact, fired by breath

Through flowering mustard
they race past a main road
northwards to the deer park

In the terrible kindness of the dead,
they whisper as they pass

Inscribe yourself if you can
on brick or bone or slate
then surrender it all with grace

Rejoice in these trees
jutting windward

A threshold
cut in rock
with seven kingdoms visible
is still no stopping place

Clouds consume the palaces
of the gods
stone chariots stir in soil
all Sarnath is covered in dirt.

There is no grief like this,
the origin of landscape is mercy.